D0064702

BEASTLY!

TIGER TERROR

Andy Baxter

Illustrations by Brian Williamson

EGMONT

Special thanks to:
Barry Hutchison, West Jesmond Primary School,
Maney Hill Primary School and
Courthouse Junior School

EGMONT

We bring stories to life

Tiger Terror first published in Great Britain 2008
by Egmont UK Limited
239 Kensington High Street, London W8 6SA

Text & illustrations © 2008 Egmont UK Ltd
Text by Barry Hutchison
Illustrations by Brian Williamson

ISBN 978 1 4052 3935 6

1 3 5 7 9 10 8 6 4 2

A CIP catalogue record for this title is available
from the British Library

Typeset by Avon DataSet Ltd, Bidford on Avon, Warwickshire
Printed and bound in Great Britain by the CPI Group

'Tiger Terror is excellent!
When can I read the next book?'
Jamie, age 9

'I liked when he turned into a tiger!'
Karl, age 7

'The stories were great because
they were full of suspense'
Liam, age 10

'Slynk stinks!'
Daniel, age 9

'Max is really cool, I really like this book'
Alfie, age 8

We want to hear what *you*
think about *Beastly!* Visit:

www.beastlybooks.com

for loads of fearsomely
good stuff to do!

MAX MURPHY Goes
from computer games
to big game in seconds

Absent-minded Uncle Herbert looks after
Max and his twin sister Molly during term
time while their parents are away.

MOLLY MURPHY
She's got brains, beauty – and a spare change of clothes for her brother . . .

Max longs for a normal family life, but that's about as likely as his uncle remembering which day of the week it is!

HERBERT SPLOTT
Otherwise known as Uncle Herbert. Big on crosswords – not quite so big on following recipes . . .

Mr and Mrs Murphy are zoologists, so they're completely crazy about animals, and they're busy working on creating the best animal encyclopedia ever. Max thinks they're weird; who wants to stand around staring at sloths when you could be tucked up at home watching telly?

MR MURPHY AND MRS MURPHY
Very bright, but a little bit bonkers!
And completely clueless about
Max's secret . . .

PROFESSOR SLYNK
Mad, bad and dangerous
to know

And, as if all that didn't make Max's life tough
enough, his parents' sinister colleague Professor
Preston Slynk has found out his secret. Slynk's
miniature insect-robot spies are never far away . . .

TIGERS: The Facts

They're hungry! Tigers are carnivores (meat-eaters) and like to feast on deer, pigs, cattle, antelope and pretty much anything else they can catch. They've even been known to chase and kill elephants. A fully grown tiger can eat the weight of an average ten-year-old boy in one go!

They're stripy! Experts think tigers' stripes act as camouflage, helping them to hide from their prey. And those stripes are completely unique, just like human fingerprints. Plus, it's not only their fur that's striped; their skin's stripy, too!

They have huge claws! Tigers' claws can grow up to 5 centimetres long. A tiger's footprint is called a 'pugmark'.

They're hefty! The heaviest tigers are Siberian tigers, the largest of all the big cats. The adults weigh in at around 225 kilograms.

They have big, scary teeth – even when they're babies! In fact, tigers have fully developed canines by the time they're 16 months old.

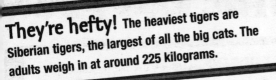

They're loud! A tiger's roar can be heard from over 3 kilometres away.

They can see in the dark! Tigers' night vision is six times better than that of humans.

INDIA: The Facts

- Its the seventh largest country in the world
- The capital city is New Delhi
- Its weather ranges from hot sunshine to very heavy rain, depending on the location and the time of year

- 17 different major languages are spoken there, and there are 844 dialects
- Project Tiger was launched in 1973 to protect Bengal tigers, and has become one of the most successful wildlife conservation ventures ever!

Contents

1. *Passage to India*

Max kept his eyes closed and tried to block out the horrible sounds coming from outside his bedroom. A shrill scream tore through the air, almost making him jump right out of his skin.

'If you don't get a move on we'll miss the flight,' shrieked Max's twin, Molly. 'You've got two minutes before I break the door down!'

Max opened his eyes and swung his legs out of bed. His left foot landed in the uneaten remains of

the supper Uncle Herbert had made him the night before. He shuddered as something green and slimy squidged between his toes. Even for someone as odd as his uncle, broccoli-flavoured ice cream was a whole new level of weird.

Max stood up and wiped his foot on the carpet. The T-shirt he'd slept in had some food stains down the front, but he reckoned he could get another day's wear out of it. He pulled on the jeans he'd left lying on the floor, looked longingly towards his games console, and headed for the door.

'Red light! Red light!'

Molly and Max stared in horror as Uncle Herbert craned round in his seat and flashed them a confused look.

'Where?'

'The road!' Max yelped. 'Watch the road!'

'Ah, yes!' Uncle Herbert exclaimed, turning round and yanking the wheel just in time to stop the car hitting a startled pensioner. 'I'll get the hang of this one day!'

The old car spluttered and screeched as it swept across two lanes of traffic and on to the slip-road leading to the airport. Half-a-dozen horns honked angrily nearby.

'Just so you know,' swallowed Max, 'when I said I didn't want to go to India I didn't mean I'd rather die instead.'

'Oh, I'm not that bad!' insisted Uncle Herbert, his gaze focused in his rear-view mirror. 'In fact, that car behind has just done exactly the same thing!'

Max and Molly turned and peered out through the layer of grime which covered the back windscreen. Just a few cars behind, a black vehicle was weaving in and out of the traffic, easily keeping pace with their uncle's old banger. A familiar face poked out from behind the steering wheel, instantly recognisable, despite an enormous fake ginger beard. A shiver travelled the length of Max's spine as the driver's cold eyes fixed on his.

'Professor Preston Slynk,' he spat.

'Rhymes with "stink",' Molly chanted out of

habit, unable to hide her disgust.

'I don't understand why you don't want to go,' Uncle Herbert continued, unaware of the drama unfolding behind. 'You might see tigers!'

'We saw tigers in Siberia,' shrugged Molly, as she and Max turned their backs on Slynk's car.

'Ah, but those were Siberian tigers,' their uncle beamed. 'These would be Indian tigers!'

'What's the difference?' Molly asked.

'Well the Siberian tiger,' Uncle Herbert began, his voice quiet as if he was revealing some great secret, 'lives in Siberia, while the Indian tiger does not.'

'Are we nearly there yet?' asked Max, ignoring his uncle's ramblings. The smell of burning rubber poured in through the car's air vents as Uncle Herbert screeched to a stop, flinging Max and Molly sideways in the back seat.

'Yes,' he grinned. 'We are!'

Max sighed and lowered his comic. Molly's bony elbows were digging into him every few seconds as she wriggled in her aeroplane seat.

'Stop fidgeting!' Max snapped. 'I'm trying to read *Space Ninjas Must Die* and watch the movie version at the same time. It's hard enough without you putting me off!' On the small screen mounted on the headrest in front of Max's seat, a Space Ninja met a messy end. 'See? I missed another good bit!'

'We've been sitting here for six hours doing nothing,' Molly protested. 'Don't you want to get up and move about?'

'Not particularly,' said Max. He popped a cheesy crisp in his mouth and crunched it noisily and fixed his eyes on the screen.

Four rows behind, Professor Slynk scribbled in a small notebook, jotting down every word the children said. From where he sat Slynk couldn't see either of the twins, but he *could* see his small robotic spy, which clung by its spindly legs to the locker above Max and Molly.

Slynk grinned. He could hear them loud and clear. It'd only be a matter of time before they gave away some secret that would help him ensnare the boy. At last the power would be his to command!

'I can't believe Stink's on board,' Molly's voice hissed over Slynk's earpiece. The professor winced. How did they know he was here? He looked down at his bright yellow Hawaiian shirt and ran his short, stubby fingers through the enormous beard which covered most of his face. The disguise was perfect, they couldn't have seen through that. It must be the boy's animal abilities. Curse them!

'I know!' Max replied. 'How could they let anyone on a plane wearing a shirt as hideous as that?'

Slynk seethed as the sound of the children chuckling crackled in his earpiece. His face turned redder than his beard.

'Enjoy it while you can,' he snarled. 'You won't be laughing long.'

'Anything to declare?'

'Yes,' announced Max. 'My sister's a pain in the butt!'

The security guard glared down at Max. Behind him the words *Welcome to Jaipur Airport* had been painted on the wall. But the guard wasn't welcoming at all. 'Move along,' he sighed, waving the twins through the security gate. They didn't look much like international terrorists. The next guy, however, was another story.

'Excuse me, sir,' droned the guard. 'Could I examine your bag?'

Slynk's eyes darted nervously from the guard to the twins, who watched with interest from beyond the gate.

'My bag?' he winced, knowing he was carrying some seriously suspicious electronic equipment.

'That's right, sir.' The guard held out his hand and Slynk reluctantly passed him the leather case. The clasp gave a *thunk* as the guard flicked it open and peered inside. 'Are you aware, sir, that your bag contains tiny blocks of metal with legs?'

'Well,' snapped Slynk, 'they're a little more sophisticated than that!' The guard stared at him, eyes narrowed. 'Th-they're robotic insects,' Slynk stammered. 'I use them to track animals. For my research.'

Molly gave a gasp and glanced across at her brother. He nodded. He was thinking exactly the same as she was: Slynk had brought the gadgets to try to capture Max. 'There they are,' chirped a familiar voice from nearby. Max and Molly turned and spotted their parents, Manfred and Millicent Murphy, striding towards them with broad grins on their faces. They all swapped hugs, before Mrs Murphy snatched up the twins' matching suitcases from the conveyor belt.

'No time to waste,' she said. 'Long drive ahead!'

'Preston?' cried Mr Murphy in amazement, as Slynk stepped through the security gate, clutching his bag. 'Is that you?'

'Manfred! Fancy seeing you here.' Slynk realised his colleagues were staring at his brightly coloured clothing. 'Luggage mix-up,' he lied. 'Terrible business.'

'And the beard?'

'I . . . um . . . forgot to shave,' he said, then quickly changed the subject. 'I've just nipped out here to film some tigers. To study their movements for my latest robotics research.'

'Then come with us!' gushed Mrs Murphy, much to Max's dismay. 'We're heading out to Ranthambore. Plenty of tigers there!'

'Oh, I couldn't possibly . . .'

'Nonsense,' insisted Mrs Murphy. 'You're coming and that's final!'

2. Something Stripy in the Shrubbery

Max fell backwards on to the couch and let himself sink into it. When Mum had said they had a long drive ahead she wasn't kidding. A four-hour bumpy jeep ride later and here they were finally at their destination.

'Sallah's prepared rooms for everyone,' Mr Murphy announced. Sallah was an old friend of the Murphys', who had invited them to stay during their visit. 'Kids, you were going to have your own rooms, but now Preston's here I'm sure you won't mind sharing.'

'No *way*!' shrieked Molly in horror. 'I'm not sharing a room with Max! He smells like a warthog!'

'Well, at least I don't snore like one,' Max retorted, throwing in some pig noises for added effect.

'If it makes things easier,' interrupted Slynk, as he sidled his way into the sitting room, 'I could share with young Max.'

'That would be a great help,' nodded Mrs Murphy. 'It'd put a stop to this silly arguing, at least.' Max stared at his sister, a hint of panic in his eyes.

'No,' Molly sighed, 'it's fine, I'll share with him.'

'Excellent, that's that then,' beamed their dad.

'But if I wake up stinking like a warthog, there'll be trouble!'

Before Max could reply, Sallah called for

everyone's attention. Their host was an expert on the area and knew all the dangers it concealed. When he spoke you listened, unless you wanted to end up as something's breakfast.

'We've got reports of poachers in the park,' he said, gravely. 'Dangerous ones. Everyone keep a look out, and if you see anything suspicious come and tell me right away.'

'Roger that!' saluted Mr Murphy.

In the corner of the room, Slynk's eyes glinted wickedly as an idea struck him. A thoroughly, wonderfully nasty idea. Perhaps capturing the boy wouldn't prove so difficult after all!

'Stop pacing and go to bed,' Molly whispered. 'It's the middle of the night!'

Max continued to wander around the

bedroom, nervously chewing his fingernails. The silvery glow of the full moon cast shadows across the walls, giving the room a spooky feel.

'You think I'm enjoying this?' Max asked. 'You think I like being on my feet when there's a perfectly good bed going spare?' He jabbed his thumb in the direction of the door. 'I can't go to sleep as long as *he*'s out there, can I? One of his robots could slip under the door any second!'

'Block up the gap then.'

Max stopped and looked at his sister. He opened his mouth to speak, then closed it again. Slowly his eyes moved down to the gap between the floor and the door, where a crack of light shone through.

'Right,' he sighed. 'And you couldn't have suggested that six hours ago?' As quickly as he could, Max rolled up his dirty clothes and wedged them into the gap, blocking it completely. 'There,' he nodded. 'That should stop anything crawling in.'

Max heaved himself up the ladder and into the top bunk. His whole body relaxed as he pulled the covers up to his chin.

'Now we can finally get some sleep!' he smiled.

At that very moment, a loud hammering on the door made the twins sit bolt upright in fright.

'Wakey, wakey!' cried their mum. 'Rise and shine!'

The early morning sun crept across the sand, sending a rippling haze of heat dancing up into the air. A battered jeep roared across the open plain. Clouds of dust billowed in its wake as it sped towards the boundary of Ranthambore National Park. On board, Max and Molly clung tightly to

their seats and tried not to throw up. The fact Slynk was sitting between them didn't make things any easier.

'How did you sleep, kids?' shouted their mum from the front seat, struggling to make herself heard over the engine.

'Great,' Max called back. 'Until someone woke us up in the middle of the night!'

'Four o'clock is hardly the middle of the night!' laughed his mum. 'Besides, if you want to see tigers, you have to get up early!'

Max didn't say anything. He didn't want to see tigers. The only animals he had any interest in seeing were sheep, so he could count them and fall back asleep. He leaned his head against the side of the jeep and let his eyelids close. In no time at all he heard the soft whirring of a zoom lens.

'Stop filming me!' he demanded, opening his eyes and pushing a camera away for the fourth time that morning. Slynk directed his camcorder out at the savannah.

'Sorry, I didn't realise it was pointing at you,' he said, innocently. 'I don't know why it keeps doing that!'

'Maybe because you keep making it?' Molly suggested, leaning as far away from the professor as it was possible to be while still sitting right next to him.

'Ah, you kids,' cackled Slynk. 'I could just eat you both up!'

'Trust me,' scowled Max. He bent forwards and rested his head in his hands. 'Sometimes the feeling is mutual.'

Max didn't hear Slynk's response. Instead, all his attention was suddenly focused on the camera bag sitting at the professor's feet. There, nestled among the batteries and tapes, was a syringe, and attached to it was the largest, most deadly looking needle Max had ever seen. Slynk could only have one target for something that looked as lethal as that . . . HIM!

'And did you know,' Mrs Murphy babbled excitedly, 'that the park is home to thirty distinct species of mammal, including macaques, sloth bears and Indian wild boar? Not to mention the tigers themselves of course.'

'Don't forget the birds, dear!' chirped her husband from his place at the front of the procession. Max rolled his eyes and trudged along behind him, dragging his feet in the dust.

'Two-hundred-and-seventy-two different types, no less!' Mum sang. 'Molly, can you name any?'

'Seagulls?' guessed Molly, as she skipped along behind her mother. After two days of travelling she was enjoying the open space.

'Seagulls?!' Max snorted. 'What, special jungle seagulls, are they?'

'Yeah, well if you're so clever you name one then!' his sister snapped.

'Fine then,' sniffed Max, folding his arms. 'Budgies.'

'Excellent guess, dear!' clapped his mum.

'Ha!' laughed Max, sticking his tongue out at Molly.

'But wrong,' Mum added.

'Ha!' laughed Molly, sticking her tongue out at Max.

At the back of the group, Slynk sighed as he tried to ignore the irritating chatter. The things he had to put up with just to try to capture the boy. The sooner he ensnared him and discovered his secret the better. And the professor had already set a plan in motion to do exactly that!

Sallah stopped abruptly and held up his hand for the others to do the same. He placed a finger against his lips and nodded in the direction of the undergrowth. Max and Molly peered through the twisted knot of weeds and branches, their eyes scanning to find whatever Sallah had seen. Suddenly, deep in the shadows, something big and black and orange stirred.

Max froze. As his eyes locked on the tiger a familiar tingle began to fill his head. He felt a buzz of electricity shoot down his spine as his mouth went dry. It was happening again! He was changing, and there was nothing he could do to stop it!

3. Love Those Tiger Feet

Tiny jabs of pain were stinging Max's eyes, like 10,000 red-hot pinpricks all stabbing him at once. Tears rolled down his cheeks, welling up faster than he could blink them away. The skin on his face tightened as his tongue grew fatter in his mouth.

'Absolutely incredible!' shrieked Mrs Murphy.

Max spun on the spot, terrified his mum and the others were watching his transformation. All eyes were still fixed on the tiger in the trees for now, but he didn't have much time!

His legs felt heavy and hard to control, and it took him three tries to kick Molly. She scowled as she turned to face him, then gasped in fright. Her brother looked awful. A film of sweat covered his deathly pale face and he was wobbling slowly from side to side. He was about to change, or he was about to drop dead. It was hard to tell which. Either way, it wasn't something their parents should see.

'Wow!' Molly yelped, pointing wildly to a bare patch of ground a short distance away. 'What kind of tracks are those? I've never seen any so big!'

'Where?' her dad twittered. He darted across to where Molly had pointed, with the rest of the group following close behind. 'I can't see anything!'

Max tried to flash his sister a grateful smile, but

the muscles in his face were no longer responding normally. He managed a nod of thanks, then turned and staggered into the jungle.

Spindly branches whipped and clawed at Max as he stumbled through the trees. A loud crashing filled his head, as if an army of ants was stomping its way through his skull. Max tried to scratch an itch spreading across his arms, but his fingers wouldn't move. Instead they shrank and twisted as they pulled backwards into the bones of his hands.

He let out a growl of pain as millions of sharp, wiry hairs burst through his skin. He managed to struggle free of his clothes just as thick tufts of orange and black fur sprouted all over his body. With a *rip* his nose split and widened as his face stretched and grew. His legs suddenly buckled under the weight of his upper body, forcing him to throw out his arms to cushion his fall. Two powerful paws landed on the jungle floor with a soft thud.

The bottom of his spine began to tingle, and he managed to wrestle his head around just in time to see a long, thin tail shoot out from his backside! He tried to cry out as enormous, needle-sharp teeth burst their way through his gums. Instead a deafening roar echoed through the jungle, sending 272 different species of bird flapping into the air in fright.

Max, the boy, was gone. In his place stood Max, the man-eating tiger!

Slowly, he padded around the jungle clearing, getting a feel for his new form. Sounds bombarded him from all directions, sharper and clearer than he'd ever heard before. A rainbow of scents wafted by his sensitive nose, some pleasant, others horrible.

Despite the immense power he could feel in his tightly coiled muscles, Max was worried. As a tiger he didn't expect to have a lot of problems within the park, but the last thing he wanted was to wander into strange territory and find himself changing back into human form. He would have to find somewhere safe and lie low until he returned to normal. A few hours lounging around in the shade was just what he needed.

Max leapt easily on to a thick, twisted branch and sniffed the air. If he concentrated, the smells swirled around to form a map in his head, and he could see exactly where he was in the park. There was a town just a few kilometres to the east. He would head in that direction, find somewhere out of sight, and sleep until the transformation wore off. He let out a quiet purr of satisfaction. As plans went, this was one of his best!

With a twitch of his back legs, Max sprang out

of the clearing and into the maze of trees. He found himself easily leaping over obstacles Max-the-boy would have struggled to climb over, and was surprised at how lightly he always landed on the other side. The foliage flew by in a blur as he bounded onward. This was fun!

A strangely tempting scent wafted by, and Max suddenly realised he was hungry. Usually when he felt his stomach rumbling he'd reach for his emergency chocolate bar, but one of the problems with being a tiger was that he no longer had any pockets. For probably the first time in living memory, he wasn't in much of a mood for chocolate, anyway. Instead, he wanted to tuck into something a little more . . . *meaty*!

The undergrowth to his right rustled as a streak of black sped from the grass, squealing in panic. Instinctively, Max's bulky body twisted in mid-air, his eyes locked on a fleeing wild boar. Saliva filled his mouth and dribbled down his chops. He could almost feel his teeth tearing through the boar's warm flesh. He could almost taste the blood flowing into his mouth as he pictured himself ripping the animal to shreds.

Max's legs tensed, ready to give chase. The boar was moving fast, but he knew he could catch it with ease. A few seconds was all it would take, then he would pin the helpless creature down and take a big, satisfying bite out of –

No! Max shook his head as he fought to resist the urge to kill. Every part of his body screamed at him to hunt the boar down and feast on its plump, juicy flesh. His coiled muscles sprang him forward, demanding he give chase. Summoning all his human willpower, Max forced himself to turn and run off into the trees, ignoring his rumbling stomach.

In amongst the jungle's din, Max heard a familiar sound. He stopped on a fallen tree trunk and listened to the ripples each noise made in the air. After a few moments, he heard the sound again. His mum was nearby, and she was talking about him.

'I just wish,' Max heard her say, 'that he'd show some interest. I mean just going off like that without telling us is very irresponsible! He's missing out on the tigers!'

If only she knew, thought Max, as he prowled

through the scrub in the direction of the sound. He crept through the tall grass, and let the leaves of low branches hide him from sight. Mum and Dad walked past, still discussing their disappointment at his disappearance. Their scent was familiar and comforting. Worryingly though, it still made a pang of hunger shoot through him.

He could see Molly standing next to the jeep. He tried to call her name, but a sound that was somewhere between a roar and a yelp slipped out instead.

Molly turned, her face frozen with fear, as a furry killing machine stepped towards her and bared its teeth. She didn't realise it was her brother smiling at her. Max's heart leapt into his throat as Molly opened her mouth to scream. He had to stop her. But how?

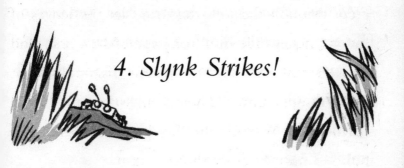

4. Slynk Strikes!

Max's mind raced. His parents would come running if Molly screamed. Worse still, so would Slynk. Molly had to be stopped before she could alert everyone.

Deep down in the most savage corners of his animal brain, he thought of one way to instantly silence her. A swift snap of his jaws and she'd be shut up for good. Luckily for Molly, the beast had not completely taken over her brother, who quickly came up with another way to show her who he was.

Molly's scream faded before it had even begun. Her terror quickly changed to amazement as the big cat raised itself on to its hind legs and fired off a perfect salute. She stepped closer and stared into the animal's face. The familiar bright blue of her brother's eyes blinked back.

'Impressive,' she admitted, as Max dropped back down on to four legs. 'Probably best you don't do that in front of any real tigers though. They might eat you.' She considered this for a moment, then grinned. 'Actually, maybe you *should* show them!'

Max let out a playful growl and gave her a shove with his paw. The gentle nudge almost sent her sprawling to the ground and Max realised just how easy it would be to accidentally hurt her.

'Watch it!' Molly warned. 'Just because your teeth are bigger than my head don't think I can't still kick your butt.' She glanced around in all directions and stepped closer to her brother. 'I told Mum and Dad you'd snuck a lift with a passing jeep and were going back to Sallah's to sleep. They weren't very impressed, but I think they believed me.'

Max nodded, then suddenly stopped. Something was wrong. A bright red mist flooded his senses. His every instinct warned him of danger. Something was about to happen. Something bad.

'My, my, aren't we a mini-Doctor Doolittle?' Slynk sneered, stepping out from behind a tree. Molly yelped as the professor clamped his hand over her shoulder, holding her in place. 'Aren't you going to introduce me to your friend?' he asked, jabbing a sausage-like finger in Max's direction. His eyes narrowed as he studied the tiger's face. 'Or have we already met?'

'I don't know what you're on about,' Molly shrugged. 'It's just a tiger.'

'What kind of fool do you think I am?' scoffed Slynk.

'A dancing fool?' smiled Molly, sweetly.

'Very funny,' Slynk said, clearly not amused. 'Let's see if you laugh at this.'

Slynk's face split into a sinister grin as he thrust his free hand into his pocket then quickly yanked out a long, thin cord which was attached to a ring of leather.

'Here, kitty,' he commanded, 'let me put this on you.' His smile quickly faded as Molly let out a loud giggle.

'A *lead*?' she cackled. 'That's your latest evil scheme? A dog lead? Maybe you didn't know, but a tiger is a member of the cat family, not the dog family.'

Max also began to laugh, though it came out

as a low, rumbling growl. It would take all of half a second to close the gap between him and Slynk, and even less time to swat him like a fly. He could win a fight with three paws tied behind his back!

'Don't laugh at me!' Slynk warned. Something about his voice made Max uneasy.

He watched as, in one movement, the professor dropped the lead and pulled the syringe from his pocket. Molly turned pale as the needle point pressed against the side of her neck.

'Now, unless you want your sister to meet with a very unpleasant end, I suggest you come over here and let me put this leash on you.' Slynk pressed the point harder against Molly's skin to show he was serious. 'Now,' he said.

Max took a few careful steps closer, moving slowly so as not to startle Slynk. He could only imagine what kind of horrible fate awaited him if he gave himself up, but there was no other option.

Even with all his speed and strength there was no way he could get to Molly before Slynk sank the needle into her neck. There was nothing else for it: if Max wanted to save his sister he had to surrender.

'That's right,' Slynk hissed, excitement sparkling behind his thick glasses. 'Come over here and give yourself up. There's a good freak.'

Molly's elbow was a blur as she fired it backwards into Slynk's flabby belly, doubling him over in pain. Gritting her teeth, she stamped her foot down on his, making sure to scrape her heel down his shin at the same time. The syringe dropped to the ground as Slynk cried out in pain and clutched at his leg. A thin trickle of blood dripped from between his fingers and thumb.

'Nobody calls my brother a freak!' Molly barked. 'Apart from me, obviously.' Max could see the fury burning behind her eyes. He was glad he wasn't in Slynk's shoes. With a grunt, Molly delivered a crunching karate chop to the professor's neck, sending him crashing face first to the ground. 'And that's for trying to hurt me!' she added, wiping her shoulder where Slynk had held her.

Max found it very satisfying watching his arch enemy rolling around on the savannah floor, groaning in pain. He felt a little silly that he'd doubted Molly's ability to look after herself. Even in tiger form he wouldn't want to mess with Molly when she was angry, so Slynk had been lucky to escape with a few minor injuries.

The smell of Slynk's blood washed over Max and made his head feel light. The red fluid oozed slowly from the scrape on the professor's leg and Max could hear every *drip, drip, drip* as it splashed against the dry ground. His stomach gave a growl of its own as the animal hunger gripped him. One bite. That was all he would take. Just a nibble. Where was the harm?

Hot drool dribbled down his chin. Maybe he'd rip his fallen foe into strips and devour the lot in one go. No one would miss someone like Slynk. If anything the world would be a better place without him. His tongue flicked across his teeth. One bite. Just one.

Molly spoke, startling him. Instinctively, his head turned and his jaws snapped at her. She let out a squeal as her brother's teeth clamped shut just millimetres from her face. Max recoiled in horror at what he'd done. The animal in him was taking over. He had to get away or no one was safe!

Max turned and ran into the jungle. He would head for the park entrance and hope he became human again before he hurt someone – or worse! Out of the corner of his eye he saw Slynk struggle to his feet and lift his arm above his head. He could hear Molly shouting, but he couldn't make out the words over the thumping of his own heartbeat. There was no way he could risk stopping to find out what she'd said. There was no saying what the beast within him would do.

A split second before Max vanished into the jungle, a small metal insect landed on his back.

Without a sound the tiny tracking device blinked into life.

'Gotcha,' Slynk smirked.

5. Spray It, Don't Say It

Max sprinted between towering trees, unaware of the bug on his back. He was trying to put as much distance as possible between himself and his family. Sure, they might annoy him sometimes, but not enough for him to want to eat them. Until he returned to normal it was safer all round for him to be well out of chomping range.

Something small and furry squeaked in terror as it scurried away, narrowly avoiding a serious squishing by one of Max's huge paws. The bushes to Max's right gave a sudden rustle as another unseen animal darted off at the first sight of the big cat. Max longed to give chase and hunt the creature down, but he knew doing that would mean letting the tiger take full control. That was a risk he wasn't prepared to take.

The further into the park he went, the more animals Max came across. Every single one – from the chattering macaques to the dozing sloth bears – panicked and fled when he approached. Max puffed out his chest with pride as a herd of wild boar scattered from his path, shrieking, squealing and falling over each other in their rush to get away. He was the King of the Jungle! Or a very close cousin, at least.

Now that he was getting used to the noise, Max was beginning to realise how effective his ears were. At first the din had been almost overwhelming, but gradually he was able to identify each individual sound, however faint it was. He could easily make out the distant snapping of branches as some of the heavier animals pushed their way through the undergrowth. Far overhead he could hear birds calling to one another. With every screech they made, a clear picture of each bird formed in his head. He didn't know their names, but he could tell from their calls alone exactly what they looked like.

If he closed his eyes and really concentrated, he could even make out the gentle pattering of insects crawling across the leaves of nearby trees. When all the sounds were combined they gave the impression that the whole park was alive, like one single, living, breathing creature made up of a billion individual parts, with Max the fiercest of them all!

Despite the noise, Max found the place very relaxing. Densely packed forest gave way to wide clearings which were dotted with lush water holes. These in turn led into ancient areas where the crumbling remains of long-forgotten buildings served as home for a wide range of wildlife. The ruins always seemed empty when Max passed, but the scents of the animals hiding inside gave them away.

Max heard a loud roar from somewhere far off through the trees. He stopped, mid-step, one paw held out before him. He recognised the sound as soon as he heard it. It was another tiger!

Max felt an overpowering urge to respond. Throwing his head back, he stretched his powerful jaws and let out a deep, rumbling roar. It felt as though the sound started deep down in his toes, then vibrated through his whole body before it echoed off across the undergrowth. He'd growled

and roared a number of times since turning into the tiger, but nothing had come close to matching the rich, booming quality of the sound he had just made. A tingle of satisfaction shot down his curved spine as the roar gradually faded away into silence.

Max cocked his head to one side and listened. Just a few seconds later, he heard the other tiger roar once more. If only he knew what the animal was saying. Maybe it wanted to be friends!

A waddling ball caught his attention as it passed across his path, unaware it was being watched. Max padded closer and sniffed the animal, then yelped in pain as a long, thin spike wedged itself in his left nostril. Down on the ground, the porcupine scrunched itself up into a small, spiky sphere and lay perfectly still.

Max staggered backwards, pawing at his face until he managed to pull the sharp quill free. His dad had warned him about porcupines, and so he knew they were not to be messed with. If he got too close he could end up with hundreds of the barbed spikes sticking into his face, and he didn't fancy that much at all. Being careful to give the porcupine a wide berth, he pressed on into the jungle.

The ground flew by beneath him as Max powered forwards, testing his body to its limits. Faster and faster he ran, his mighty muscles propelling him over, under and through any obstacles he encountered. The wind nipped at his eyes as he sped along, but nothing could slow him down. Nothing could get in his way. He was a savage, unstoppable killing machine. He had raw, animal power, and he was loving every minute!

With a grunt, Max leapt from a branch and landed atop a mound of rubble in another clearing. Before him, what must once have been an enormous monument, stood in ruins. Most of the larger stones, which made up the building, had toppled over long ago, but what remained standing was still impressive enough to take Max's breath away. From the sweeping stone staircase leading up to the top of the monument, to the massive statues standing beside its crumbling walls, everything about the construction was awe-inspiring. *Fit for a king*, Max thought, as he padded up the moss-covered steps.

Half way to the top, he stopped. A thick, musty scent caught in his throat and he felt his hackles rise. A picture of a leopard formed in his mind as he sniffed the air, and he knew the animal must recently have marked this as its territory. Not for long!

Purring with satisfaction, Max lifted a hind leg and began to spray. His own scent sloshed against the steps, quickly masking the smell of the leopard.

When he had finished, Max threw back his head and gulped in a lungful of air. His scent washed over the area, spreading out like a cloud and letting the other animals know he had claimed the monument as his own. Although he would never have listed pee as one of his top ten favourite aromas, there was something about the smell now which made him feel incredibly happy. He stretched his massive jaws again and roared with delight. This was his territory now, and nothing would take it away from him!

A low, menacing growl caught Max's attention. It was coming from the top of the steps. Up above, another tiger stood watching him, its eyes narrowed; its fangs bared. Max thought back to the roar he'd heard earlier and let out a low whimper. He still couldn't speak tiger, but now he had no doubt that this one most definitely did *not* want to be friends!

6. A Big Cat-Astrophe

Despite his strength and power, Max could almost feel himself shrinking under the tiger's glare. Every part of the big cat's body was tensed and coiled, ready to spring at any moment. Its face was twisted in a furious snarl, which showed off two rows of yellow teeth, each one capable of ripping out Max's throat.

Max took a backwards step away from the beast, trying to keep his distance. It quickly padded down the top few stairs, closing the gap between them again. If Max turned and made a break for it, he knew the other tiger would leap on to his back before he'd even reached the bottom of the steps. Running wasn't an option.

The tiger's eyes widened a little and it tilted its head to one side. It continued to stare down at Max, but now its expression looked more puzzled than angry. Max held his breath. It must have spotted his blue eyes. Maybe it would realise he wasn't a real tiger and leave him alone! Moving slowly, so as not to startle the beast, Max retreated further down the steps.

The tiger roared forwards, its fangs fully bared, its whiskers rigid. Apparently it didn't care if the newcomer was a real tiger or not. Instinctively, Max dropped down so his belly was against the cold stone steps. He lowered his gaze in an act of submission. The last thing he wanted was a fight! But the second tiger had other ideas.

A primal voice in his head screamed at Max to move. He sprang to his feet just in time to avoid a swinging blow from the tiger's paw. The fur on the back of his neck stood on end as he reared up on to his hind paws, claws extended. He could feel the animal within him pushing up to the surface, overpowering him completely. He had no choice but to give in to it. Truth be told, he was relieved to let it take control.

Another swipe swished past his face and Max felt the tips of the tiger's claws brush against his fur. Close. Way too close. The animal lunged at him, huge paws flailing wildly. The hot stench of death hit Max in the face as his opponent roared with fury. From this distance he could make out every little bit of raw flesh that was stuck between the tiger's teeth. The seriousness of the situation finally hit him. He was facing an experienced killer.

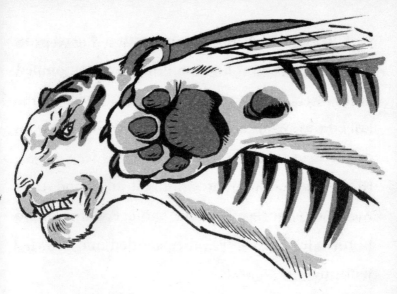

A savage blow struck Max on the side of his head, sending him tumbling backwards down the steps. Panicking, Max jumped back on to his feet and lashed out with his front paws, but he struck nothing but air. Once again he reared up on to his back legs, only to be sent sprawling as the other tiger cannonballed into his chest. The two beasts rolled end over end down the steps, snarling and swiping at each other again and again as they thudded against the crumbling stone.

They landed at the bottom with a *thump*. Max had hit the ground first and found himself pinned down by the weight of the other animal. He lashed out with his claws, pushing the tiger away, desperately trying to escape. With a deep growl, Max managed to force himself free, and they rounded on each other once more. Padding round in a circle, face to face, they snarled and growled with rage.

Now they were on the ground Max considered running into the trees. The tiger might not chase him, but if it did there was a chance he could outrun it. For a brief second his gaze shifted to an opening in the jungle on his left. Seeing its opportunity the other tiger pounced. Max heard the beast move, but turned too late to avoid a crunching blow. He roared in agony as three sharp claws ripped right through his fur and split open the skin on his shoulder. A patch of red

quickly began to spread out from the wound.

Almost at once his opponent dropped down on to four legs and took a few paces backwards. Max watched in amazement as the animal stretched, yawned, then padded back off up the steps. The tiger had wanted to show him who was boss, and he'd done just that. The battle was over. Max had lost, but he didn't care. He was relieved to have escaped with his life.

Whimpering in pain, he sped back into the jungle. There was a chance the tiger might change its mind and come back to finish the fight, and Max didn't want to be there if it did. His shoulder burned with each step he took, but he didn't dare stop until he was far, far away from the monument.

Max finally reached a shaded area where he could lie down and get his breath back. Being a tiger was turning out to be a little too exciting for his liking. What he wouldn't give to be back at home with his games console. At least there the only serious injury he could sustain would be thumb-ache!

His heart rate was gradually returning to normal, and he decided that a nap might help him to feel better. He'd be able to think more clearly after that and figure out where in the park he was. An hour or so of lazing in the shade would be enough. He gave the wound on his shoulder a lick. Although he wasn't sure why he was doing it, it seemed to ease the pain a little. He rested his head on his paws, closed his eyes and settled down to sleep.

'You're not listening to me, you idiot,' hissed a voice from somewhere close by. Max flicked his eyes open but otherwise remained completely still. There was no mistaking the unpleasant nasal whine he'd just heard. Slynk!

Cautiously, Max got to his feet and crept through the trees in the direction of the sound. The professor's rancid reek stung his sense of smell as he approached. He and Molly had been right all along – Slynk really did stink! He followed the stench until he could make out the shape of an overweight man through a gap in the trees. Slynk was standing in a clearing and talking into a mobile phone, unaware he was being watched. Hiding behind some low-level leaves, Max stopped and listened.

'It's a special tiger. Completely tame. Timid, even,' said Slynk. He rested a hand on his hip as he listened to a voice on the other end of the phone. 'Well how should I know? Maybe it was in a circus or something. Does it matter? All you need to know is that it's absolutely, one hundred per cent harmless. All you have to do is capture it and bring it to me. You will, of course, be paid well for your trouble.'

Max growled. So that was the professor's game. He was hiring some local thugs to catch him. Well, they'd have to find him first and that wouldn't be easy!

'And don't worry,' said Slynk into the phone. 'Finding it will be very straightforward, no matter where it goes in the park.' He grinned as the person on the other end of the phone asked him the obvious question. 'That's the clever part,' he boasted. 'I've stuck a tracking device to its back. You'll be able to follow its every move!'

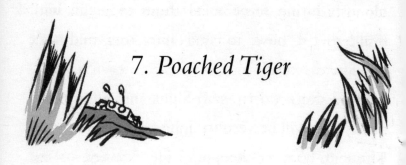

7. Poached Tiger

Slynk's words echoed around inside Max's head. He'd been tagged! He cursed himself – how could he not have noticed? That must've been why Molly shouted after him earlier. If he was to have any hope of avoiding capture, Max had to get the device off his back.

After a hasty retreat into the trees, Max twisted round to try and get a view of the gadget. It took him several attempts, but if he bent his neck as far as it would go and lowered one shoulder, he could just make out a small metallic block half way along his spine. The tracker clung to his fur with tiny legs. The blinking light on its back told Max that it was transmitting his location even now!

If he strained his ears to their limits he could make out a faint, high-pitched electronic hum. The sound had been there at the very edge of his hearing since his earlier encounter with Slynk, but he'd been too busy enjoying his new body to notice it. The device had to be removed before it led Slynk's newly hired henchmen directly to him. There was no way he could bend far enough to take it off with his teeth, so he'd have to come up with a more creative solution.

The tall grass rustled beneath him as he flipped on to his back and rolled around. He pressed his full weight down on the robotic bug and felt it digging into him just below his shoulder blades. Ignoring the pain he pushed harder against the jungle floor, grinding his spine against the tracker. The ultrasonic hum continued uninterrupted. The ground was too soft to cause the gadget any damage.

With a growl, Max leapt to his feet and threw himself backwards into a nearby tree. Again and again he rammed himself against the thick trunk, shaking it wildly each time. Somewhere up in the branches a monkey screamed in panic and clung on for dear life. The metal insect clung just as tightly to Max's fur, refusing to release its pincer-like grip. Each crunch against the trunk knocked the breath from his lungs, but no matter how hard he smashed, the bug remained intact.

A small crowd of animals had gathered at the edge of the clearing and were now watching Max in wonder. Even the porcupine from earlier – or one very like it, at least – had trundled up to see what all the fuss was about. They all stood gazing in silent amazement at Max's antics. They had never seen the majestic Bengal tiger acting like this before, and they were keen to find out what the big cat would do next.

Ignoring the assembled audience, Max charged at a large boulder sticking up from the jungle floor. Just before he reached the rock he ducked his head and rolled forwards, timing the move so his back took the full brunt of the collision. He roared in frustration when he realised the tracking unit was still firmly attached.

His every muscle ached as he launched himself against the rock once more, harder this time than before. The crash sent shockwaves of pain passing through his bones. He gritted his teeth as the wound in his shoulder split open and seeped blood down the entire length of his leg.

Perched on their rocks and branches, the gathered spectators chattered excitedly. Many of the smaller animals munched on mouthfuls of seeds and nuts as they watched the tiger's bizarre performance. They'd remember this show for a long, long time!

Max clawed at his shoulders, desperately trying to reach the bug on his back. None of his swipes even came close. He let his head hang down low and took a few moments to get his breath back. It was no use. He couldn't remove the robot. There was only one person who could help him now.

He'd have to move quickly if he was going to get to Molly before Slynk's goons found him.

The onlooking animals scattered as Max approached. He sniffed the air, trying to conjure up another mental map of the area. The quickest route to his sister would be back the way he had come, but that would mean crossing paths with the other tiger again. There was a good chance it might not let him off as lightly next time, and he didn't want to risk another injury.

Max padded in a different direction, trying to picture another way to reach Molly. If he travelled east for a few hundred metres, then turned southwest, he could probably be there in a little under . . .

Suddenly a sharp, stinging pain shot through his paw, making Max yelp with fright. Fearing he'd stepped on something poisonous he tried to back away, but found himself tethered tightly by the leg and unable to move. A length of nylon cord was wrapped around his ankle. With every move he made, the rope pulled tighter, and already he could feel it digging into his flesh. Still he pulled, gritting his teeth against the pain, as he fought to be free of the trap.

He stopped pulling as loud, humourless laughter echoed from the jungle. Max watched in horror as four scruffy men dropped down from nearby trees and slowly began to approach him. They each had wide, toothless grins on their faces, and three of them carried thick, heavy-looking sticks. The fourth man held a gun, which he was aiming at Max's head.

A thousand thoughts raced through Max's mind. Were these Slynk's men? No, they couldn't be. Slynk's men wouldn't even have arrived yet, so there was no way they could have set up a trap like this. These must be the poachers Sallah had

warned them about!

He would have been relieved that Slynk's men hadn't caught him, if it wasn't for the fact that his dad had told him exactly what poachers did to the tigers they caught. They'd start by beating him to death. While he was still warm they'd skin him and tear the teeth out of his head. They might even rip out his bones if they thought they could find a buyer for them.

The men continued to laugh as they approached – it was an oily, sickening cackle that made the fur on Max's neck stand up. They jabbered to each other in a language he didn't understand. He didn't need to know what they were saying to understand what they were about to do though. The way they gripped their thick wooden branches told him everything.

A fury like none he'd ever felt before welled up from deep down inside Max as he eyed the poachers. As a tiger he might be one of the most savage beasts on the planet, but these were the real predators. They'd waited until their prey was helpless before making their move. They were the animals here, not him.

A red mist of rage clouded his vision. His blood boiled in his veins. He roared loudly, startling the poachers. Bucking and twisting in a ferocious frenzy he heaved at the cord, barely feeling the pain as it cut deeper into him. But the pain didn't matter. Nothing mattered except being free. Then he'd make the poachers pay. He'd make them all pay!

8. Rumble in the Jungle

A deathly silence had fallen over the entire area, broken only by the occasional growl from Max as he wrestled with the rope around his ankle. The harder he pulled, the tighter the trap became, but he continued to struggle, determined to break out. The tiger had almost completely taken over. He could no longer think clearly. All he could do was heave and tug and fight with all his might to be free.

The tiny part of his mind that was still his own

was fighting another battle. He had to regain control. There was no way he could break out of the trap with brute force. That would only make things worse. He had to get a hold of himself if he wanted to make it through this alive.

Max gulped in deep lungfuls of air. *Slow and steady*, he told himself with each big breath, *slow and steady*. Concentrating hard, Max managed to lessen the pace of his pounding heart. He could feel the fog lifting from behind his eyes. His body suddenly came under his control again. He'd done it! He'd calmed the raging beast!

Max dropped to his belly and studied the noose around his leg. There had to be a way out, and if he could just think about it, calmly, he'd be sure to find it. Other tigers might be as strong as him – maybe even stronger – but none of them could use reason and logic like Max could. If a human brain could come up with the trap, then his human brain could escape from it. He just needed a little bit of time.

The poachers had stopped talking and were standing watching him in amusement. Their weapons hung limply by their sides. No doubt they would soon remember why they were there. Any second now they'd move in for the kill. Max couldn't tell whether the head poacher's gun was

loaded with bullets or tranquiliser darts, but it didn't make much difference. Either way the final result would be the same. If his luck didn't change soon he'd be a tiger-skin rug by the end of the day.

Max pushed the image from his thoughts and focused all his attention on the trap. Now that he studied it properly the answer was actually quite simple. The good news was that he could see a way to escape. The bad news was he'd need thumbs to do it, and right now thumbs were two things he just didn't have. One of the men raised his stick above his head and took a careful step closer. Max gulped. This was it then. He was well and truly done for!

A loud rustling off to the right caught everyone's attention. Some dense bushes were pushed apart, making room for three large men to come charging through. Max could hear the quiet bleeping of the small hand-held computer the first man carried. They were following a tracking device. These must be Slynk's men. *Oh, great,* thought Max, *as if things weren't bad enough!*

The poachers turned and squared up to the newcomers, shouting at them in a language Max couldn't understand and waving their sticks threateningly. Slynk's men shouted louder and waved even bigger sticks back at them. Within seconds tempers had flared and everyone seemed to be screaming at everyone else. Max couldn't understand a word, but judging by the way both groups kept pointing over at him he was an important part of the argument. They were each trying to claim him, he realised! They were arguing over who had first dibs on the captive tiger!

One of Slynk's men strode across to Max, chattering angrily every step of the way. He barely paid the tiger any attention, as he reached down and fiddled with the complicated clip of the tracking device from his back. The henchman turned to the poachers and held the robotic bug up for them to see. His thick moustache bristled as he gave a triumphant grin. As far as he was concerned the tracker proved that Max belonged to him and his two companions.

The poachers stared right past him, their jaws hanging open. They'd never seen anyone approach a tiger so recklessly and live to tell the tale. All four of them gripped their weapons tighter, fully expecting the trapped animal to launch another crazed attack. Max remained completely still. Slynk's hired men obviously believed he was completely tame and harmless, so he'd let them carry on believing it. He'd wait and see what was going to happen next before making any moves. If he was lucky, he might be able to make a run for it while they were all arguing. If he was *very* lucky both groups might wipe themselves out and he'd be free to go. Either way, he'd play it cool for now.

The poachers began to protest loudly as the man with the tracking device took out a collar and tied it around Max's neck. Max even turned his head to one side, helpfully, to let the henchman attach a chain lead to the collar's metal clip. It seemed no stronger than the one on Uncle Herbert's bath plug back home and wouldn't prove a problem if Max decided to bolt. One sharp movement of his head and he'd be able to break it in half.

Max held his breath as the man gripping the lead pulled a large knife from the side of his boot. Ignoring the angry shouts of the poachers, the man knelt down, took hold of the cord, which held Max in place, and sliced it clean in half. The pain in Max's paw began to ease almost immediately. He felt just about strong enough to make a run for it.

The hired goon gave the lead a sharp yank and Max slowly got to his feet. The poachers let out loud shouts of panic as they stumbled backwards away from the beast. In their rush to flee, they smacked into Slynk's other two men, knocking them to the ground then tumbling down on top of them. Slynk's men cried out in anger and quickly moved to wrestle the poachers off.

Max watched in amusement as the fallen men became a flailing mass of arms, legs and sticks. Everyone seemed to be swinging wildly, and not really caring who they were hitting. The man holding Max's lead was shouting and stamping his feet. No matter how loudly he shouted, however, nobody seemed to be listening.

The man muttered something under his breath and led Max over to a tree. Still mumbling, he wrapped the lead around a branch and stormed into the fray. The polished blade of his knife glinted as he held it out before him. Max watched the man pull one of the poachers to his feet and wave the knife in front of his face. The poacher went cross-eyed as he tried to focus on its sharp blade.

Somewhere, off to his right, Max heard a metallic click. He whipped his head around and found himself staring down the barrel of a gun. The lead poacher grinned, revealing a mouth full of black, broken teeth. He squinted slightly as he peered along the gun's sight, which was focused right between Max's eyes. He might not be getting the tiger, but there was no way he'd let these other fools take it alive!

The poacher snarled something Max didn't

understand. Half a second later he squeezed the trigger.

A single gunshot roared through the jungle.

9. The Beast Unleashed

Max slowly opened one eye and peered around the clearing. He was alive. That was unexpected, but a welcome surprise. The trigger-happy poacher was wrestling with one of Slynk's men, who was trying to tear the gun away from him. He must have knocked the gun off target. *Of course! Slynk wants me alive*, thought Max. *I'm no use to him if I'm dead.*

With a grunt, the poacher pushed his attacker away and raised the gun again. Max heard the soft *click* of a bullet entering the firing chamber. He saw the tendons in the poacher's hand tighten around the trigger. There was no one to save him this time. There was nothing else for it.

Max's savage roar drowned out the *bang* of the gun as he leapt at the poacher. The bullet whizzed over his head, well wide of its target. The chain holding him in place snapped as easily as he'd expected it to. He heard the man screaming with horror as the angry beast moved towards him. It was a deeply satisfying sound.

The full weight of Max's tiger form thudded on to the poacher, knocking him to the ground. The gun was sent flying through the air before it disappeared into the thick undergrowth. Max pressed his paws down on the poacher's arms, pinning him like a butterfly.

Max growled down at his captive as he thought of all the other animals this man and his

gang must have killed. He imagined all the ways they'd have made the poor creatures suffer. Max's thick tongue flicked over his yellow teeth. Now it was their turn.

A large piece of wood knocked against Max's head. He span round quickly, sending a second poacher stumbling backwards against a rock. In one swift movement, Max snatched the stick out of the man's hands and bit clean through it. Two short pieces of timber landed quietly on the jungle floor. Max snarled at the poacher, fury burning behind his blue eyes. He took a step away, making room for the man to run. He wanted him to run. He wanted them all to run!

As the poacher made a break for it, Max roared triumphantly. In two massive bounds he was on the man, pushing him face first into the damp ground. The man opened his mouth to scream, but a muffled squeak was all that emerged. Thick claws ripped at the poacher's heavy jacket, tearing it to shreds. Max's face twisted into a mask of anger.

The clearing filled with screams of panic. The poachers and Slynk's men tripped over each other as they tried to escape into the depths of the park. The man Max had pinned to the ground began quietly to sob into the moss.

The snarl faded from Max's face. He wanted to keep clawing at the man's exposed skin. He wanted to make sure this man never hurt another living creature again. But he wouldn't. He wasn't an animal. He just looked like one from time to time.

Still, that wasn't to say he wasn't going to give the men the fright of their lives! Roaring, snapping and snarling, Max bounded around the clearing, knocking them over one by one. Each time he sent a man sprawling, he took a few moments to growl in his face, letting long strands of saliva drip down upon him. When he'd finished terrifying one man he'd move on to the next and give him exactly the same treatment. He didn't want any of them to feel left out, after all.

When all the men had been suitably scared, Max bounded off towards the edge of the park. Hidden by the trees on the outside of the clearing, he hesitated and looked back at them. They were slowly getting to their feet, but they all looked like they could fall back over at any second. He grinned a toothy grin as he watched them tremble and shake. Maybe now they'd think twice before harming any more animals.

Once the poachers realised the tiger had finished with them, they ran off as fast as their legs would carry them. But Slynk's men weren't so quick.

'Now I've got you!' cried Slynk, as he burst out

of the jungle and into the clearing. Max ducked down low and watched to see what would happen next. Slynk waved the giant syringe above his head. In his other hand he clutched a tracking computer, which was bleeping excitedly. His gleeful expression sank as he glanced around at the shaken, dishevelled men. Max was nowhere to be seen. 'Where is it then?' he spat. 'What have you idiots done with my tiger?'

The group turned on Slynk, angrily. Their pride – among other things – had been wounded, and they wanted to take their frustration out on someone.

'*Your* tiger?' asked one of the men in broken English. Max recognised him as the one who had pulled the tracking device off his back. 'The one that you say will not hurt a fly?'

'Yes!' Slynk snapped. He was getting impatient and didn't seem to notice the man's growing resentment. 'Now I demand that you tell me where he is!'

The man slowly stooped and picked up one of the sticks from the ground. All around the clearing the other men did likewise. They moved to form a ring around Slynk, blocking his exit.

'You know, I'm not sure,' the hired hand shrugged. 'I lost track of him after he tried to *eat my face off*!'

Slynk swallowed nervously and lowered his arm. It finally dawned on him that he was completely surrounded by a group of very angry men who were armed! It also occurred to him that it was largely his fault that they were so annoyed. Moving as one, the men advanced.

'Now, chaps, no need for any trouble, is there?' Slynk whimpered. 'I thought it was completely safe. I thought it was tame! How was I to know it would get violent?'

'Violent?' snarled one of his men. 'We'll show you violent!'

Max watched through the branches as the men began to swing at Slynk with their sticks. The professor hopped around in a circle, looking for a way to escape. For a moment, Max almost felt sorry for him. Maybe he should leap back in there and save him from the beating? He could scare the men away with a single flash of his claws . . .

Nah!

'Get off! Cut it out!' yelped Slynk, bobbing and weaving around the clearing. Max watched him, silently.

Suddenly, Slynk stumbled to his knees and let out a yelp of pain. The men gathered round him, beating their sticks on their hands menacingly. As Slynk struggled back to his feet, Max noticed something dangling from his right thigh. Slynk had fallen on to his own syringe, and the serum inside it was seeping into his leg.

Slynk tugged at the syringe and just managed to yank it out before falling, face first, to the ground.

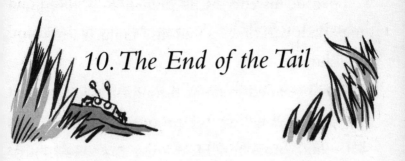

10. The End of the Tail

Max threw back his head and laughed. Out in the clearing everyone froze at the sound of the roar. Slynk's men all began to scream again, convinced the tiger had returned to finish them off. Only Slynk knew the truth. He seethed quietly as the laughter rebounded through the trees and came at him from every direction. *One day,* thought Slynk, *one day I'll get my revenge!*

The scents of the jungle swirled in Max's head, combining once more to form a detailed map of the area. The trees became a blur and the wind whipped at his ears as he launched himself into the park. It was time to find his family. It was time to go home.

Max bounded joyfully through the jungle, his paws barely touching the ground as he flew over rocks and branches. He'd miss this. He'd miss everything about being a tiger. He'd miss the power. He'd miss the enhanced senses. He'd even miss the stripes. They were a good look for him. Still, he consoled himself with the fact that tigers couldn't play computer games. They couldn't spend entire Sundays in bed watching DVDs and eating chocolate either. Being a boy had its advantages too!

With a grunt, he propelled himself out of the woods and on to the dry, barren plain. He hit the ground awkwardly, tumbled over his legs and rolled sideways in the dirt. He had been sure-footed since the transformation. Why was he stumbling now? Suddenly a familiar tingling crept across the back of his head. He was changing back!

Off in the distance, he could make out the jeep they'd all travelled in just a few hours ago. His parents and Molly would be nearby. He struggled to his feet and loped off in the direction of the vehicle. He had to get back before he changed completely. This was no place for a lone boy to wander. There was nothing in the park that would eat a tiger, but he was sure there were a few things that would happily gobble up a child!

Running was getting more and more difficult. Max could feel his paws shrinking and changing shape. Before he knew it he was crawling along the savannah on his hands and knees. Then, like a sprinter off a starting block, he hurried on, pulling himself upright mid-run. His tiger teeth stung his gums as they pulled back into his head. All over his body he could feel pinpricks of pain. The thick fur that had covered him was rapidly retracting into his skin.

Max looked down at his now mostly human body. His skin was bruised and filthy, with a patch of dried blood covering most of his injured arm. He would have a lot of explaining to do, but first he had to find some clothes!

A few moments later Max staggered up to the jeep, fighting to draw breath. The effort of running had made his every bone ache. He felt light-headed, and like he was about to throw up. There was no doubting it – he was a boy again.

He rummaged in the back of the jeep until he found Molly's rucksack. Undoing the zip he thrust his hand inside, praying she'd remembered to bring his spare clothes. His fingers found a crumpled T-shirt and a pair of battered jeans, and

he breathed a sigh of relief.

Within seconds he'd pulled the clothes on. He wriggled his feet into a scuffed pair of trainers just in the nick of time.

'Max!' shrilled Mrs Murphy, her voice filled with concern. Max looked up as his mum and dad darted over to him with Molly in hot pursuit. 'What on earth happened?'

'I . . . er . . . hitched a lift,' he explained, thinking as quickly as he could. 'But they turned out to be poachers.'

'Poachers!' his dad gasped. 'I say, that's rotten luck!'

'You're sure they were poachers?' asked Sallah, as he joined the group. His expression was very serious.

'Positive. They told me they were tiger watching, but I spotted their snares in the back of their jeep. When they realised I knew what they were up to they attacked me and left me in the middle of the park.'

'Oh, my poor boy!' Mum shrieked. She threw her arms around Max and hugged him protectively.

'Those ruffians!' said Mr Murphy, punching his fist into his hand. 'Sallah, this must be reported at once!'

'Right,' Sallah agreed. 'We'll go back into town and get some of the other guides together.' He rested a strong hand on Max's uninjured shoulder. 'We'll get them, young Max. You have my word.'

Max nodded. He didn't doubt Sallah for a second. He was glad the poachers would be rounded up and punished. They certainly had it coming.

'Perhaps we should find Preston first,' Mrs Murphy suggested. 'Professor Slynk wandered off earlier and we haven't seen him since. You haven't come across him on your travels, have you, Max?'

Max tried to hold back a smile, but couldn't. Molly saw this and broke into a grin of her own.

'You know,' smirked Max, 'I can't say that I have.'

'Sounds like you had a pretty wild time,' Molly whispered. Max sat next to her on the jeep's back seat and closed the door behind him.

'It was amazing,' he told her, talking quietly so his parents and Sallah couldn't hear. 'I was snared, tied up, shot at – I even got into a fight with a real tiger!'

'Really?' Molly gasped. 'Who won?'

'I'd call it a draw,' Max lied. 'But I could have taken him if I'd really wanted.'

'Yeah, right,' laughed Molly. 'I bet he whupped

you good and proper!'

'Speaking of being whupped, look over there,' Max said, pointing to a gap in the trees just a short distance from the jeep. Molly turned in time to see Slynk stagger from the jungle, with a strange smile on his face and a faraway look in his eye. He was caked in mud and animal dung and seemed to be having difficulty walking in a straight line. Max and Molly glanced at each other, then erupted into a fit of giggles.

'Preston, don't tell me you were kidnapped by poachers too!' Mrs Murphy quizzed. She and her husband ran to Professor Slynk's side and each took an arm to hold him up.

'Poachers? What? Where?' the man babbled. He tried to make a run for the jeep, but his legs buckled under him and he fell to the ground.

'What were you doing wandering around the jungle on your own anyway?' asked Millicent.

But Slynk seemed to be in a world of his own, 'Nice, tame tiger. Here, kitty, kitty,' he jibbered.

'You should know better at your age!' Millicent continued, tutting to herself.

Opening the back door of the jeep, Millicent and Manfred shoved Slynk on to the seat next to Max.

Mum, Dad and Sallah all took their seats in the front. The engine roared as Sallah turned the key, and Slynk almost jumped out of his skin.

'Are you OK, Professor Slynk?' asked Molly, sweetly.

'I'm fine,' said Slynk, slumping forward in his seat, as the jeep roared off.

'It's been a long, tiring day,' Max grinned. 'I'd imagine he's just well and truly *beat*!'

Off in the distance the other tiger let out a rumbling roar. Max felt a twinge of sadness. Despite everything, he'd enjoyed his time as a

tiger, and was glad he'd been able to stop the poachers. He'd grown to like the park and its many residents and wished he'd had more time to spend there. Suddenly, his normal life didn't seem quite so interesting.

Still, his adventures as a tiger might be over, but he had a feeling there were lots more adventures yet to come. Not today, though. He'd had quite enough for one day.

Smiling to himself Max leaned his head back against his seat, closed his eyes and drifted off into a long-overdue sleep.

More Terrific Tiger Facts!

They're rare! Though, thanks to the efforts of wildlife protection groups, the world tiger population has now grown from around 4,000 in the 1970s to an estimated 6,000. Still, there are three times as many tigers in captivity as there are in the wild.

They're not all the same you know! There were once eight different kinds of tiger. Three of these – the Javan, Caspian and Bali tigers – have become extinct in the last century, and now only the Bengal, Sumatran, Siberian, Indochinese and South China tigers remain.

They'll never be pensioners! In the wild, tigers live about 10 to 15 years. In zoos, they have a lifespan of about 20 years.

They're chilled! Tigers don't like the heat and prefer to hunt in the very early morning or late at night.

They love water! Unlike most cats, tigers enjoy cooling off in water and are strong swimmers.

They're athletic! Tigers have been known to leap over 10 metres in a single bound.

They enjoy catnaps! Like most cats, tigers love to rest. They can often sleep for 20 hours in a day.

ONLY JOKING!

What do you get when you cross a guard dog with a tiger?

A very scared postman!

On what day do tigers eat?

Chewsday!

How do tigers describe themselves?

Purr-fect!

How does a tiger greet people?

Pleased to eat you!

WHAT KIND OF WILD CAT ARE YOU?

Native Americans believe we each have a speci[al]
connection with a certain type of animal. Try th[is]
quiz to find out which wild cat you're most like .[..]

**Choose the shapes next to the statements
you agree with:**

- ■ I'm very calm and don't have a bad temper
- ▲ Sometimes you just have to do things without thinking too much
- ■ I find it hard to sit still!
- ● I find it easy to concentrate at school
- ▲ I'm never late
- ● I'm a very fast runner – one of the fastest in my class!
- ▲ I'm always rushing around
- ■ I'm one of the strongest people in my class

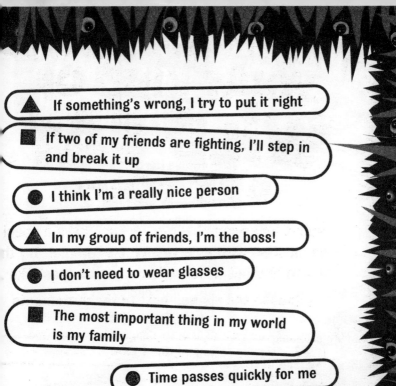

▲ If something's wrong, I try to put it right

■ If two of my friends are fighting, I'll step in and break it up

● I think I'm a really nice person

▲ In my group of friends, I'm the boss!

● I don't need to wear glasses

■ The most important thing in my world is my family

● Time passes quickly for me

SCORES

▲	●	■
If you chose mostly TRIANGLES, your inner wild cat is a **TIGER**. You're:	If you chose mostly CIRCLES, your inner wild cat is a **CHEETAH**. You're:	If you chose mostly SQUARES, your inner wild cat is a **LION**. You're:
Strong	Clever	Cool
Up for anything	Focused	Love being at home with your folks
Lively	Fast	Physically powerful
Reliable	Confident	Brave
(Nearly) always right!	Busy	Full of energy

UNCLE HERBERT'S TASTY TIGER TOAST

Uncle Herbert's original version of tiger toast used baked beans and black treacle, but we persuaded him that you'd find this one much tastier!

YOU'LL NEED:

2 slices of bread

Some grated orange cheese

Brown sauce in a squeezy bottle

A grown-up helper

HERE'S WHAT TO DO:

1 Wash your hands

2 Ask your grown-up to help you grill both slices of bread on one side only

3 Place the slices on a plate, toasted side down

4 Sprinkle on the orange cheese

5 Squeeze some stripes of brown sauce over the top (see photo)

6 Ask your grown-up to help you grill again, until the cheese bubbles

7 Let your tiger toast cool down, then eat!

Try making a sweet version using marmalade and chocolate spread!

Yum!

Can't wait for the next book
in the series?
Here's a sneak preview of

SHARK SHOCK

1. Party Pooper

'I can't believe you aren't excited!' Molly cried, as she and her brother made their way towards the school gates. 'Think about it! We could go snorkelling. Or scuba diving, even! Wouldn't that be brilliant?'

'Aren't snorkelling and scuba diving the same thing?' Max asked, although he didn't really care about the answer. It was the last day of school before the summer half term, which should have been cause for celebration. He'd planned to spend the whole holiday completing *Ecco the Dolphin* – a new console game he'd ordered – with his best friend, Jake. Unfortunately, his parents had other ideas, and he and his twin sister, Molly, had both been booked on a flight to . . . to . . .

'Where is it we're actually flying to again?'

'Cartagena in Colombia,' Molly sighed. 'How many times do I have to tell you?'

Max shrugged. 'Until I stop asking.'

'I think they play football there, too!' continued Molly. She was skipping now, the way she always did when she was excited. 'Maybe we can get a game!'

'Oh, you think so?' said Max, sarcastically. 'Whoopee!'

The fact was the only thing he'd hate more than playing a game of football was a playing a game of football in Colombia. It wasn't that he had anything against Colombia in particular, it was just that he'd far rather be sitting at home watching a game of football on telly. Most of the time he hated having jet-setting parents. Today, though, he *really* hated it.

'Shame we'll have to miss the party at Samreen's house tomorrow, though,' Molly admitted. 'That would have been great!'

'I'd forgotten about that!' Max yelped. 'Oh, this just gets better and better doesn't it? So, I'm missing out on the party of the year *and* intensive computer sessions with Jake, for what? Two weeks at a . . . a . . .' he hesitated. 'What is it again?'

'It's Malpelo Island Flora and Fauna Sanctuary. We're catching a private plane there from Colombia,' tutted Molly. 'Try to pay attention!'

Max stopped in his tracks. 'Wait a minute,' he said, 'flora and fauna – that's plants and flowers and stuff, isn't it? Mum and Dad are zoologists; they study animals, not plants! Why are we going to look at flowers?'

'Fauna means animals,' Molly explained, rolling her eyes. 'I thought everyone knew that!'

'I knew that, I was just testing to see if you did,' Max fibbed. 'Now come on. We're going to be late for school.'

Max dunked his last chip into his blob of tomato sauce then popped the whole thing in his mouth. All around him the canteen was filled with excited chatter about one thing and one thing only: Samreen's party.

'Shame you can't come,' said Jake, who was sitting directly across the table. Jake was Max's best friend and the only person, apart from Molly, he'd shared his secret with. 'Just about everyone is going to be there. It's going to be awesome.'

'Yeah, well . . .' Max began.

'Samreen's mum and dad make the best food,'
Jake drooled. 'There's usually loads and loads of it
too. There's always tons left over!'

'Yes, thank you, I get the picture,' Max sighed.
'I feel bad enough already!'

'Oh, yeah, sorry,' Jake said. 'Still, you're going
to Colombia!'

'Don't remind me!' said Max. 'Apparently they

have lots of,' he shuddered as he said the next word, '*activities*.'

'What, like computer games?'

'*Physical* activities.'

'Oh, dear,' replied Jake. 'What are you going to do?'

'As little as possible, hopefully,' Max said. 'It's like they say, you can bring a boy to Colombia, but you can't make him scuba dive.'

'They don't say that,' Jake laughed.

'They will by the end of next week,' grinned Max.

'I hear you're not going to make it to my party,' said Samreen, as she sat down next to Jake. Molly walked up with her and sat next to her brother. Both girls put their dinner trays down on the table. Straight away, Max began to pick pieces of food from his sister's plate. 'That's a pity, it's going to be great!'

'So everyone keeps telling me,' Max nodded.

'My mum and dad have been cooking since Wednesday!' Samreen told him. 'We'll probably end up having to throw most of the food in the bin if you're not going to be there.'

'Really? That's a– hey, what's that supposed to mean?'

'She means you eat like a horse,' Molly explained. She jabbed her brother on the hand with her fork as he reached for one of her potatoes. 'Now leave my lunch alone!'

'Where is it you're going this time, anyway?' asked Samreen. Max shrugged and glanced at his sister.

'Colombia,' said Molly. 'It's going to be so great. We're going to go snorkelling, aren't we Max?'

'Well, you might be,' Max replied. 'But if you think I'm setting foot in the water you've got another thing coming!'

'Why not?' sneered an all-too-familiar voice from over Max's shoulder. 'I thought you'd be right at home down there with all those spineless little sea sponges!'

The twins turned and looked up into the grinning face of Stewart Staines. Stewart spent break times going round the school making the lives of other kids miserable. Max sighed. Was it his turn again so soon?

'All right, Brain Strain?' Max nodded.

'I told you,' the bully seethed, 'never call me that!'

'Sorry,' smirked Max, 'it must've slipped my mind.'

'Did someone mention a party?' asked Brain Strain hopefully. Samreen sighed. She hadn't invited Stewart. 'It's a real shame you're going to miss it,' Stewart continued. 'I'm sure it'll be much

more fun than mucking around with a load of stinking sea sponges!' He leaned down so his face was next to Max's. 'Apparently they're the smelliest creatures in the sea. Nothing else that lives down there will even go near them, that's how disgusting they are!'

'Why are you going on about sea sponges?' asked Max.

'You get them around Colombia,' said Stewart, trying his best to sound intelligent. 'Saw it in a documentary last night.'

'Right,' snorted Max. 'And when you say "documentary" do you in fact mean "cartoon"?'

Brain Strain opened his mouth to answer, but the bell rang for the end of lunch and stopped him in his tracks.

'We'll finish this later, Murphy,' he spat, before storming off out of the dinner hall.

'See you later,' said Molly to Max, as she and

Samreen got up from the table. Jake began to move, but Max held his arm.

'D'you know if Brain Strain's right?' he asked. 'About sea sponges?'

'No idea, why?'

'I might change into one!'

'Oh, yeah,' Jake winced. 'That would be horrible.'

Max nodded. Changing into a sea sponge *would* be horrible, and there was no way of knowing if it was going to happen. He didn't know how his transformations worked. All he could do was wait and see.

The smelliest creature in the sea, he thought. *Won't that be just my luck?*